CHAPTER ONE

Addy couldn't let them catch her. Not now, not ever. That single thought in mind, she clutched the small bundle in her arms tighter and forced herself to run faster. Her inner lioness attempted to help, adding what strength and speed she could, but it wasn't enough. They were larger, stronger, quicker, and fueled by both rage and fear. She'd managed to avoid them for the last two weeks, but the more time that passed, the closer they came and this was the closest yet.

She still wasn't sure what clued her in to their arrival, but something alerted her lioness danger was near. She'd peeked out the front window of the moldy hotel room, spied the two hulking males, and then escaped out the back with nothing more than the clothes on her back, a diaper bag, and what those two men hunted... the baby.

She ducked and weaved through the busy crowd, fighting the natural flow of foot traffic. She took advantage of the fact she was much smaller than the two males. At over six feet tall and two hundred-plus pounds, they had to struggle against the gathered bodies.

Growls chased her, their sounds making it seem they were within inches of her, but that couldn't be. She'd had a decent lead when she fled the hotel, hadn't she? Now snarls reached her, the men foisting their anger at her actions. The humans' fear stung her nose as they seemed to finally realize they had furious non-human somethings in their midst.

They were livid with her, but they couldn't have known why she'd run. Then again, maybe they did and didn't give a damn. They worked for Tony Davis, didn't they?

And Tony wanted his baby back.

Not while she had breath in her body.

"Dammit, bitch."

"Fucking catch her."

The two men's words reached her, syllables sending forward a new panic that threatened to freeze her in place. Thankfully they instead served to spur her on and she dug deep for any remaining energy.

Can't be caught... Can't be caught...

Little Jack whimpered and released a low cry, reminding her why she pushed so hard. For him. For his future.

"Shhh... I have you. I'm going to take care of you. Be easy, sweetheart." She tried to soothe him without missing a step. Any hesitation, any bit of slowing, would result in her capture.

And not just capture, but also her death.

Unacceptable.

Jack whined again, telling her exactly how upset this mad dash was making him. She would have to calm him. Later. Right now, pure adrenaline drove her onward.

She could almost feel their breath on the back of her neck, the moisture of their spittle landing on her skin, and she clawed deeper inside herself. She increased her pace, changing her movements from quick ducks and dashes to outright shoves. She pushed others out of the way, ignoring their surprised shouts. There was no time for apologies or requests. Only running.

Addy glanced at street signs as she darted through intersections, fighting to remember the layout of the massive city. She'd only been in town a month and all that time, Tony's drivers/bodyguards escorted her everywhere which meant she still didn't know her way around.

Yet another crosswalk loomed before her, the curb crowded with early morning employees hoofing it to work. She glanced at the "walk" sign and noted it still told walkers it wasn't safe, but—she glanced over her shoulder and trembled in fear—they were too close.

Addy burst through the clumps of people, racing dead center through the mass and straight out the other side. She glanced down the street, trying to gauge the oncoming traffic. Yells followed her, but she was in a straightaway. She could make it through the intersection and on to the other side before her pursuers—or the approaching cars—reached her.

"We're almost safe, sweetheart. Almost safe," she whispered. Addy made it past the bicycle lane, knowing she was putting more and more space between her and the men. She made it past the first lane as well. "Almost—"

She didn't make it past the second. A high-pitched squeal of tires was the only warning she received that her world was about to be destroyed once again. She only had a split second to spy the source of that sound, to watch a big vehicle bear down on her. The grill grew closer and closer, the auto seeming to be aimed directly at her, and she distantly wondered if one of Tony's goons were behind the wheel. But why would he risk his own son?

Then the question became moot because the SUV wasn't going to stop in time. Addy's lioness whined in anticipation of the coming pain, and she twisted in place, making sure the grill struck her back and not little Jack.

She wrapped herself around him, desperate to cushion him from any harm as the vehicle plowed into her. Pain exploded in her back and then it enveloped her entire body. Her shoulder snapped out of place and she recognized when her arm broke, but still she kept Jack protected. She hugged him close, arms carefully shielding him from the rough ground as it scraped skin from her body.

The coppery tang of her own blood filled her nose. That scent was joined by the oil and rubber that coated the road. It was then she realized she'd stopped rolling. She was no longer skidding over the ground and remained motionless.

The baby's wail filled her ears, the child announcing its fear to the heavens with an ever-increasing volume. Agony wracked her body, assaulting her from within, and she knew she had to have broken more than one bone. Her only hope now was that her lioness could help her shake off the injuries—heal her enough so she could stumble away without being caught. She'd have time to recover once they were safe.

Screams and questions were thrown at her, the stench of the crowd's worry burning her nose as people tried to discern if she was okay and what had happened.

No, I'm not okay. I got hit by a fucking truck.

But she didn't put voice to those words. Instead she concentrated on her beast's attempt to heal the damage to her body. The bones would be crooked, there was no hope for that, but she could worry about re-breaking them and setting them correctly once she found a new place to hide.

She forced her eyes open, anxious to see where her pursuers lingered, and she found them at the edges of the wide circle that surrounded her. Both men glared at her, their golden eyes seeming to bore into her, and a new wave of fear crashed over her body. She had to go. Had to run.

She glanced down at Jack, running her hand over his tiny form, and she ignored the agony that came with the movement. He appeared no worse for wear, and she sighed in relief when she realized he was unharmed and only scared.

A loud thud reached her, the sound close and obviously from a vehicle, and then a male she didn't know crouched at her side. His eyes were the yellow of a lion, and a light dusting of cream fur coated his tanned cheeks. Finding a lion at her side was not surprising in a city filled with her kind. However, finding the lion at her side was also her mate floored her. His scent was deep and smoky, offset by the aroma of the dry plains that imbued every werelion, and it called to Addy's cat.

Her inner beast purred and whined in relief, soothed by his presence. He would protect them, he would take care of them, he would... He would keep Jack safe. At least she hoped.

His gaze stroked her, enveloping her from head to toe, and her inner lioness was calmed even further by his attention and worry.

"It's you," she whispered and frowned. Why was her voice so thin and reedy?

His irises seemed to glow even brighter as he stared at her face, and he revealed his possessiveness with his first utterance. "Mine." His nostrils flared as he breathed deeply, and his attention darted from her face to the rest of her. "Where are you hurt?"

"I'm fine." She lifted one hand from Jack and placed her palm on the asphalt, intent on rising from the street. She shouted with the first new bolt of agony that struck her with the pressure. That was echoed by his roar of rage and it had the crowd making a rushed retreat.

"Where are you hurt?"

Where wasn't she hurt? Not only that, but she was finding it harder and harder to keep her eyes open. Her eyelids grew heavier by the second and darkness crept into her vision until the world was coated in a gray cast. "I'm…" She shook her head and struggled to dispel the dizziness that attacked her. "I'm…"

"Fuck."

"Don't… Curse… Around the baby." The stench of her own blood filled her nose, and she realized two things. She was bleeding freely from a wound and her cat still hadn't managed to stem the flow. That meant she was quickly losing consciousness. She was going to pass out, leaving herself vulnerable… Leave Jack vulnerable. Addy shoved back the darkness long enough to reach for her mate, to grasp his hand despite the agony that struck her, and demand his attention. His worried gaze met hers. "Don't let them take the baby."

"The baby?" Confusion filled his features and his focus flicked to the squirming bundle in her arms and then back to her.

She had to get him to do as she asked, had to get him to listen to her.

And so she lied. "Don't let them take *my* baby."

*

Zane was torn between snatching the wriggling child from her arms before the baby tumbled to the ground and catching her before her head struck the concrete. It was obvious she was rapidly losing consciousness. She had a lioness but the inner beast wasn't healing her. Why? Even though he'd hit her with his SUV, she should have been well on her way to recovering and not still bleeding all over the road. That only happened when a lion was severely weakened. From exhaustion? Hunger? Stress?

It wasn't only the scent of her inner cat that prodded him, but also his lion was more than intrigued by the female. In fact, he was pacing in the back of Zane's mind, digging his claws in deep and scraping at him. It demanded to be released so it could chase off the crowd that surrounded them. It wanted to protect and care for its… Mate?

Mate.

That realization had a new tension thrumming through his body. There were too many people nearby, she was hurt, and she demanded that he care for her child. *Her* child. The feline inside him snarled at the thought that another had touched her, another had given her a cub. Any children she had would come from him.

Once again the lion made demands, encouraging him to dispose of the baby that wasn't of his blood. The cat was ruthless and violent and it didn't care they were half human. Didn't give a fuck that humans didn't kill the children of other males. It demanded Zane recognize that he was part lion as well and their kind destroyed any remnants of others.

He battled to keep the beast under control and snarled at the animal, shoving it to the back of his mind and tying it to the shadows. They had other issues to deal with at the moment.

Such as the fact their mate was quickly fading. As her head dropped to the ground, he slid his hand beneath her and kept her from harm. At the same moment, her grip slackened and the child almost fell as well.

"Zane, what's up?" Oscar yelled, and several grunts followed the words as the massive lion pushed his way through the gathering.

"Take the baby." He was quick to issue an order. "I've got the mother."

The moment Oscar removed the child, Zane swung the woman into his arms. He fought to ignore the whimper and moans that followed the movement, the rush of moisture—her blood—that coated him.

Once again his lion attacked. This time it wasn't demanding he get rid of the cub but was furious they'd caused their mate pain. There would be a lot more agony before all was said and done and that pissed it off even more. Not much he could do about it though. He recognized more than one bone had been broken when the truck had struck her, and the gouges and scrapes were still bleeding heavily.

He spun toward his SUV, ignoring the people who shouted at him, telling him to call an ambulance and not to move her. They didn't understand. They didn't realize at this point he *needed* to get her medical care and—for a shifter—that wasn't necessarily at a hospital. They also didn't understand that if they didn't get the fuck away from him, he'd kill them all. This woman—the stranger—was his *mate* and they needed to back off.

Unfortunately the crowd still seemed intent on delaying him. Rather than pushing them aside or asking them nicely to get out of his way, he merely roared. Except there was no "merely" about it. He let his beast come forward, let it transform his vocal chords until a full-grown, enraged lion roar echoed off the buildings surrounding them. The acoustics amplified the sound until every human in the vicinity ducked and cowered beneath his rage.

Yes, every *human* hit the ground, but two males still stood. They were both large, towering above the trembling masses. Their gazes were intent on Zane, eyes hidden behind dark glasses, but he sensed their malice and barely banked rage. Then that focus shifted from him to Oscar and by extension the child. Their body language changed, fury transforming to near desperation.

It didn't take a rocket scientist to see the two males were the "them" and they were the ones who wanted the child—his mate's child.

Not happening.

Zane pushed his way through the fearful crowd and went straight for his SUV. Oscar stood at its left, still cradling the small child and shooting him a look of pure confusion. He didn't have time for explanations. Not that he knew anything worth sharing. What he *did* know was his mate needed care and the longer his fellow enforcer held the baby, the louder and more upset it became.

"Get in the back with the kid."

"Wha—"

"I don't have time to argue with you, Oscar. Get in the back with the baby. Be careful with it. I'm gonna strap her into the passenger seat and then we're going to my place." The pride doc could help her better than a hospital emergency room. Ignoring his friend, he stepped around the door that remained ajar, and carefully slid the woman onto the leather seat. He ignored the stains of blood swiped across the pale leather. He would have time to hate himself for injuring her later. Right now, he needed to remain focused on getting her help.

It took seconds to get his mate strapped in and then he stepped away to slam the door only to find Oscar still standing nearby. "What the fuck? Get in the fucking back."

"Look, man, you need to tell me what the hell is going on."

Zane's lion leapt forward, bristling at the challenge to his authority, and suddenly his fangs were extended and bared at the male. His fingers and hands were now deadly paws and claws, and golden fur coated his arms. "Get. In the fucking. Car." He noted movement over his friend's shoulder and glared at those two males attempting to approach them from behind. "Now."

"Zane—"

"I got my fucking mate bleeding in the front seat and that's her kid. So listen to me, for fuck's sake." He really didn't have time for this shit.

"All right, man. Why the fuck didn't you say so?"

Zane was gonna kill the lion as soon as he was sure his mate was safe.

Oscar climbed into the back, carefully holding the little tike, and Zane glared at the two men who still stood nearby. That menacing air continued to surround them and he ached to wipe the floor with them. They wanted his mate's kid? They'd have to go through him first.

There was nothing his lion hated more than big guys picking a fight with somebody smaller. It didn't get any smaller than a baby. And as much as his lion disliked the idea that she'd been with someone else, it despised the prospect of those two goons getting their hands on the little one.

He shot a glare at the males and was gratified when they both tensed and twitched. Yeah, they were big and strong, but Zane was meaner.

It didn't take him long to round the vehicle and slide behind the wheel. It took even less time to start the engine and throw it into gear. A single long press of his horn disbanded the gawking group, and then he was rolling down the streets once again.

Zane pressed a button on the steering wheel to initiate a call, and the moment it was answered, he barked out his orders. "I want the pride doc at my place in three minutes. I got a mom and cub in my car that need help. Tell him the mom has been hit by a car."

"Zane?" There was no way to miss the Alpha Mate's confusion. "What are you—"

He tried to be nice to her, he really did. He'd been running an anti-dick campaign since his beta, Brett, mated Jennifer. He'd been a dick to the lioness then and now he was trying to clean up his act. But fuck if he could be diplomatic now. "I have my mate in the passenger seat of my SUV and she's bleeding everywhere, Penelope. Get the damn doctor to my apartment. I'll be there in two minutes."

"Why aren't you taking her to the hospital?"

"With all due respect, Alpha Mate, get the doctor to my fucking apartment." He pressed the button to end the call and focused on driving. If he took the shortcut and raced down 4th, he could shave ten seconds off his time. Since the doctor lived in the same high-rise as him and damn near the rest of the pride, he knew the male would be waiting for them when they arrived. So the quicker Zane got there, the quicker his still nameless mate would get help.

"Zane... Marcus isn't going to be happy with you talking to his mate that way." Oscar wasn't lying.

The only thing he could do was hope the pride alpha saw Zane's side and knew he'd been worried about his mate when he was so disrespectful to Penelope.

"Hold on." He took the corner hard, ignoring the squeal of the tires as he whipped onto 16th.

The building was in sight and he pushed his way down the street, disregarding red lights as he raced down the road. He came to a screeching stop and vaulted from the SUV to race around the vehicle. Other pride members released shouts of surprise and more than one growled at his sudden appearance. Yeah, he pissed off a lotta people in general. Today was nothing new.

Zane snared the door's handle and yanked, giving himself access to the passenger seat. Before he leaned over his mate, he caught sight of those two guys once again. This time they were seated in a non-descript black sedan, parked south of the building and tried to appear as if they hadn't tailed him through a mad dangerous dash through the city. They wanted her. No, they wanted the baby and that made him even more determined to keep the kid safe. He was a contrary fucker.

"Get the baby inside and up to my place," he growled at Oscar and then focused on taking care of his mate. With infinite care, he undid her seatbelt and gathered her into his arms once again. The red stains were large on the seat, sinking into the pristine leather, and his lion roared its objection at her continued bleeding.

Without hesitation, he held her close and whirled toward the building's entrance. Oscar was on his heels as he raced into the high-rise and his fellow pride members were quick to give him a path to the elevator. One of the other enforcers—Austin—held the door wide.

"Take care of my truck, will ya?"

"Sure, Zane." The male was quick to answer.

"And there're two lions in a town car down the street. Big, mean looking fuckers and they want my cub. *I* want them gone."

Austin's surprise was instantaneous at the mention of a child but he quickly recovered. "Consider it done."

Assured in his new family's safety—for now— he refocused on his mate. The second he stepped into the elevator, Oscar pushed a button to close the doors and then they were heading up to his floor. Quiet surrounded them, making his worry grow since he hardly heard his mate breathing. All that broke through the quiet were the low cries from the baby fussing and whimpering and that simply added to his animal's fury. His mate was hurt, his baby was upset, and those two assholes...

"You know you're gonna have to clean up your language. You got a kid now."

For a bare second his worry was snatched away from his mate and he focused on Oscar. The lion merely turned his head and gave the blank and unblinking stare as he waited for Zane's response. And Zane... had only one thing to say to the male.

"Fuck. You."

CHAPTER TWO

Addy woke with a rush, slamming from unconsciousness to fully awake in less than a heartbeat. As she opened her eyes, a scream erupted from her throat and she gasped for air. Fear, a familiar emotion, attacked her the instant she scanned her surroundings. The walls were clean, the room smelled fresh, and there was no hint of decay marring the carpet.

It wasn't a place she knew nor did it look like somewhere she could actually afford.

The rapid, heavy thump of booted feet pounding on a solid floor hit her ears a bare second before the door was busted down. The wood panel went slamming against the wall, a foot to the lock easily shoving the door from its frame. The owner of that foot strode into the room, and his golden-eyed gaze swept the area in one rapid glance.

Fury emanated from every line of his body, from the tenseness in his mouth to the ever-widening breadth of his muscular shoulders. His arms were flexed and his human hands resembled lion claws. He was massive, well over six feet and easily more than two hundred fifty pounds of enraged werelion. The only thing that kept her from collapsing into a tearful puddle was that his anger wasn't directed at her. In fact, it seemed to be hunting the cause of her fright.

And then those orbs focused on her, the amber flaring even brighter as his stare slid over her in a gentle caress. When he didn't find anything physically wrong with her, he seemed to expel the anger in a single exhale. His lion gradually retreated, leaving tanned skin as fur receded and green eyes when the cat completely vanished. He drew in a deep breath, nostrils flaring as he inhaled, and then he released it with a deep purr.

Oh.

Addy did the same, scenting the air, desperately searching for the male's natural flavors and her heart stuttered at what she found.

Her mate. She gasped. *Her mate.*

Now? She discovered her mate *now* when she was running for her life; running for Jack's life.

Jack.

Addy yanked at the blankets covering her, shoving and tugging on them, unsuccessfully battling to rid herself of the restraints. "Where is he?"

Her mate frowned. "Who?"

She growled and bared her fangs, but her head was now wrapped in the sheet, totally killing the effect. "Jack," she snapped. "Where is he?"

He narrowed his eyes. "Who the hell is that? If it's some ex of yours, you can forget about him. You're mine."

Seriously?

"Look, I don't know who you think you are…" Addy finally got the sheet from around her and gave it one last yank, freeing her fully. She carefully pushed herself until she was sitting on the edge of a… bed? Yes, she was in a bed. In a bed and no longer wearing the ratty jeans and worn t-shirt she'd donned that morning. Now she was clothed in a baggy top and equally large drawstring shorts. Her grimy sneakers were gone, and her hair was no longer tied in a ponytail at the base of her skull. Basically, she looked nothing like she had when she'd rolled out of bed.

With a shake of her head, she tried again. "Look, I don't know who you think you are, but—"

"I'm your mate."

"—you need to tell me what you've done with Jack."

He narrowed his eyes and a whisper-quiet growl thrummed through the room. "Don't you growl at me," she hissed. "I've eaten bigger lions than you for breakfast. Give him back to me and then I'm leaving."

"But," he blinked in surprise, "you're my mate."

"And he's only a baby. One who needs my protection. That comes in the form of getting him the hell out of here." She braced one hand on the mattress and slowly pushed to her feet. She swayed slightly, knees unwilling to help her stand, and she stumbled to the side, grasping one of the bed's post to keep her upright.

"You can hardly stand," he snarled.

"You don't have to stand to ride a train."

"Dammit. Sit down before you fall down. How the hell are you gonna take care of a cub if you can't even get out of bed?"

He had a point. Not that she was telling him that. "I need to leave."

Leave before Tony's guys found her. Before they crashed into wherever the hell she was and snatched the baby from her arms.

"No, what you need is to relax for thirty seconds so we can talk."

The man didn't realize stubborn was her middle name. "Look—"

He growled at her, the only warning she received before he darted forward and pulled her into his arms. He cradled her close and was gentle despite his large size and obvious anger. One giant step had them beside a plush chair, and another had them both cuddled in the cushioned center.

"No, you look. We're going to talk and you're not going anywhere until we do."

Addy snarled. "That's kidnapping."

"You're my mate. That's like stealing a car I already own. Ain't gonna happen."

That had her bristling. "So I'm a car now? Is that a dig because I've got a wide ass?"

Self-conscious lioness, party of one.

His brow furrowed, mouth forming a small frown. "I like your ass. Not that I looked when I changed your clothes. But you were hurt and somebody had to take care of you and the fucking doctor had already fucking had his fucking hands all over you. I was gonna fucking kill him."

"I don't even want to know." She shook her head. "We're getting off topic here. Where is Jack? Is he okay?"

"Is Jack the baby? That's his name?"

She didn't want to give him any more details than necessary, but answering one question would lead to another which led to another and then the eventual revelation of the truth. And then they'd make her let him go.

"Yes, my baby's name is Jack."

He eased her closer, arms holding her the tiniest bit tighter, and she fought the desire to simply sink into his embrace and take comfort in the feel of his skin on hers. Except she couldn't afford a distraction. Not now, not ever.

"But we both know Jack isn't your child. So why don't you answer my questions and then we can talk about what the hell is going on."

It all sounded so rational. Too bad she wasn't prepared to listen.

"He's mine," she growled.

He shook his head. "No, he's not." He sighed. "How about we start with your name? Mine is Zane Edwards. I'm one of the North American pride enforcers."

A new jolt of terror overtook her, blinding her to any good sense. Without thought, she struggled against his grip, fighting to get free. She would find Jack on her own and then run as far and as fast as she could. He was an enforcer. *Enforcer.* His job was to uphold the laws. Which Addy had blatantly broken when she'd fled Tony's. It didn't always matter that a person had good intentions.

"I-I-I—" She couldn't get out any other words, her mind overrun by panic. Not for herself, but little Jack and what would happen if his father got his hands on him. Her best friend's voice—Jack's mother—drifted through her mind.

If Jack stays with him, Tony will kill him. This life will kill him. I want more for my son than an existence of stealing or hurting others and dodging bullets or claws from the pride. You have to help him...

"Hey, shhh..." He stroked her back, large palm tracing her spine and she figured he was probably trying to calm her, but his touch did anything but. "It's okay."

No, it was very *not* okay. "I have to go. I want Jack and then I want—"

"Hello, I see my patient is up." Yet another stranger poked his head through the doorway, his gaze bouncing between Addy, her mate, and back again. "How are you feeling?"

"Patient?" She raised her eyebrows in question.

The man came forward and she recognized the tools of a doctor's trade; the ever-present stethoscope and white jacket making his profession easily identifiable.

"Patient." He tugged the stethoscope from around his neck. "You were one injured little cub when Zane carried you in here." He pressed the cool pad of the stethoscope to her back. "Deep breath for me." She did as asked, repeating the move several times until he finally stepped back. "Any pain? Anything still bothering you?"

"I'm fine. I need to see Jack." Why wouldn't anyone listen to her?

"Well, *that* is up to your mate and the alpha, but I can tell you he is healthy as can be and doing fine. Didn't even have a scratch on him after your adventure with your mate's car."

Addy only distantly acknowledged that apparently she'd been hit by a car while she still held Jack in her arms. Even more, her mate was apparently the one who'd been driving. That news was frightening, but sheer unadulterated terror struck her when she realized the North American Alpha was now involved in the situation.

"Can-can—" she licked her lips, "can I see him, please?"

She needed to see him, touch him, and make sure he was okay. And then… Then she'd snatch him and try to figure out where to go. Her lioness whined an objection, aching to stay near her mate rather than going on the run. But she had to think of more than herself, of the promise she'd made and the small life that hung in the balance.

The doctor frowned. "I believe Alpha Marcus wants to speak with you first."

Of course he would. Of course he had questions, ones Addy didn't want to answer. But she didn't get a chance to tell him. The male simply turned on his heel and strode toward the door, leaving her alone with Zane once again.

"I don't want to talk to him. I want Jack and then I'll get out of your lives." She didn't miss Zane's low growl and she also didn't miss the way her inner cat responded with an interested purr.

"You're mine. *Mine.*" He tightened his hold slightly, but not enough to jostle her injuries. "I'm not letting you go. I'm not letting Jack go."

I sliver of hope drifted into her heart. "You won't—You won't let anyone take him away from me?"

"Us." He cupped her cheek and encouraged her to meet his gaze. "I won't let anyone take him from *us*."

"There's… He's not… I took…" How did she explain the truth?

"I know you're not his birth mother. Everyone who has come in contact with both of you knows this. Did you break any laws—human or shifter—to have him? You have to tell me."

A tremor racked Addy and she wasn't quite sure how to answer the question, but she tried. "In my heart, *I* don't believe I did, but others might think…"

"Then the answer is no. Jack is yours, you are mine, which means Jack is mine and I'll be damned if I let anyone take what belongs to me."

For the first time in weeks, for the first time since her best friend's brutal death at Tony Davis' hands, Addy was able to breathe.

*

With those quiet words, Zane's mate shuddered and relaxed against him as tension fled her body. She might not trust him, might be filled with panic and fear, but she at least accepted those few words as truth.

"Now that you know I won't let anyone take him, why don't you tell me what the fuck is going on?" He internally winced, knowing the way he worded the question wasn't exactly classy.

She chuckled, and the teasing sound turned into a low groan that had his beast hissing within his mind. "It might be better if you don't know all the facts."

"Nope, not gonna work. Tell me already."

"Bossy," she grumbled. "I am Adelaide Wilson, but my friends—correction friend—call me Addy. Or rather, she did before…" She swallowed hard and blinked back her tears. "I'm just Addy."

Zane traced her lower lip with his thumb, staring at her mouth and wondering what she'd taste like. "Addy. I like that. Addy and Zane." He was tempted to brush a soft kiss across her lips, but kept himself in check. "And Jack?"

"It really is best if you don't know." At least then he could claim ignorance and maybe Tony would take it easy on him for helping her.

"Maybe you let me decide that."

"No…"

"I can't protect you and Jack if I don't know." He tucked a few errant strands of hair behind her ear and ignored the way she shook her head and continued to deny him. "How about I guess then?" He didn't wait for her agreement. Instead, he simply told her what he'd worked out so far. "He's not yours, Addy. I think he belongs to one of the guys who chased you out in front of my truck. Am I right?"

Zane waited for her lie, held his breath as he anticipated the untruth to drip from her lips. She was in trouble, scared, and still hurting, so he couldn't blame her if she continued to lie. He hoped she would soon trust him. Actually, he wanted to yell at her and shake her, demanding her to have faith in him right this moment. But he didn't let his usual uncontrolled anger take over.

"I didn't give birth to Jack, but that doesn't mean he's not mine." She snarled the last few words, revealing how much she cared for the baby. "And no, neither of those men fathered him. His dad couldn't even be bothered to think of him until he was missing."

Her fury assaulted his nose with a burning heat, and it was tinged with a giant heap of terror. He gently ran his hand along her back, tracing her spine and trying to soothe her. He hadn't ever had experience calming someone, but there was the first time for everything. "Okay… Can you tell me anything else? *Will* you tell me anything else?"

She remained quiet, nibbling her lower lip as she met his gaze and then turned her attention elsewhere. He knew he was being judged, Addy trying to figure out if he could be trusted, and his lion snarled at the fact she didn't blindly believe in him the first moment they met.

The front door to his apartment opened and then softly thumped closed, which was followed by a low murmur of voices. She stiffened in his arms, a new wave of fear slid through her so he increased his soothing attentions. "Addy?" He prodded. "Are you going to talk to me?"

Look, he even made it a question and everything. Those voices drew closer and he was easily able to pick apart the owner of each. Marcus had obviously come, and the other male was his brother and pride beta, Brett. The tinkling feminine laughter from Penelope and Jennifer was joined by a baby's giggle. They would soon have a full house, five more bodies crowded in this room.

"You need to give me something before they get here."

"I…" Her eyes clashed with his and he couldn't fail to notice the moisture gathered there. The way it threatened to overflow and cascade down her cheeks. "I…"

Dammit. He wanted to growl and snarl at her, intimidate her into telling him the truth, but he bit back the sounds. She was already hurting both emotionally and physically, and he had no doubt she was utterly exhausted.

Who knew how long she'd been on the run and hiding? Who knew how long they'd been on her tail and dogging her steps? For her to go running into traffic… They were definitely dangerous.

Zane brushed her hair back from her face and cupped her cheeks, wiping away the first tear that trailed down her face. "I'm going to take care of you. You and Jack, okay?" She carefully nodded and he leaned forward to press a gentle kiss to her forehead. "Good. Stay here, and I'll be back."

"But what about…"

"You don't worry about anything." Yet another droplet of moisture escaped her eyes. "You're my mate, Addy, you know that right?" At her nod, he continued. "So I'm going to take care of you. You rest for a little bit and I'm gonna get Jack. The doc already checked him over and someone went and got everything we'll need for him. You both take it easy and I'll deal with everything else."

Disbelief and hope warred and fought their way across her features. "You'll… But you don't…"

Zane rose, taking her with him. Keeping her cradled in his arms, he carefully padded toward the bed and gently laid her on the soft surface. "I'll take care of you, and for now, I know everything I need to know."

He dropped a kiss to her forehead once again, pausing long enough to take a deep breath and savor her delicious scent. He wanted her, he ached for her, but it was obvious she was in no shape to welcome him.

Besides, it seemed he had a mess to deal with. Someone wanted his mate and the cub. He simply needed to find them and explain that Addy and Jack weren't their concern any longer. Whether that was with words or claws, he didn't know and honestly didn't care. Actually, he had a good bit of anger currently directed at himself and he wouldn't mind blowing it off on one of those goons.

"I'll be right back," he murmured against her skin.

"O-okay."

Zane forced himself away and moved to the closed bedroom door. He carefully opened it and slipped into the hallway, stopping the approaching group before they neared the room. He held up a hand, palm out. "I need the baby and then I'll talk to you guys in the living room."

Marcus—his alpha—raised a single brow. "You will, will you?"

Fury, not unlike what he ached to direct at the two men who'd scared the hell out of his mate, filled him. "Yes. I won't have my mate upset. She's dealt with enough. All she wants is her baby and then she needs to sleep. You're going to let her."

It was nonnegotiable.

"Your mate?" Marcus' other eyebrow joined the first in surprise.

"Yes," he bit off.

Marcus gave him a speculative look. "All right, for now I'll accept the claim, but I need to speak with her. The baby doesn't belong to her. You know that."

Zane's shoulders tensed, the hair on the back of his neck raising as his lion bristled with his alpha's words. "She's my mate and she says the baby belongs to her. Ergo, the baby is mine. I want him."

Brett snorted. "*Ergo.*"

Zane finally got the chance to snarl and bare his fangs at another beast. Brett responded with aggressive sounds of his own and Zane's skin rippled with his inner lion's anxious need to burst forward. He'd been craving blood from the moment he lifted Addy into his arms, and it seemed he'd finally get his wish.

"Marcus?" Penelope's soft voice sliced through the anger that filled the air, and the alpha sighed and slumped his shoulders.

"Enough. For now, questions can wait."

"And Jack?" Zane was not moving an inch without the cub. The look on his alpha's face told him the male did not want to hand Addy the child when it obviously did not belong to her. They didn't share a scent, not even a hint of one that would tie them together as family members, let alone the shared flavors of mother and son. "I want him, Marcus."

Penelope sighed. "Marcus, it's not like she can leave the apartment without anyone seeing. There's only one way in or out."

Zane wasn't about to tell the Alpha Mate she was wrong and that he'd had a little something added to his place.

Penelope continued. "It's obvious she loves him—she wouldn't have nearly died for him otherwise—and he won't stop fussing. He's going to make himself sick if he doesn't calm down soon."

"Fine," the alpha growled. "But I expect answers and I'm going to get them."

Marcus would get something, but it would only be what Zane was willing to give him and nothing more.

CHAPTER THREE

Addy cuddled little Jack close, smiling into his bright blue eyes. He greedily sucked on the bottle, swallowing down the formula while keeping his attention entirely on her. He looked so like his mother, even now at such a young age his features resembled Addy's best friend.

"Oh, Lori, I wish you could see him," Addy whispered and then pressed a soft kiss to Jack's downy head. "But I'm keeping him safe for you. I won't let Ton—" she swallowed the man's name before she could put voice to it. Lions had excellent hearing, and the last thing she wanted was to expose her secret. "I won't let him get hurt."

Jack released the nipple, his lids fluttering closed as sleep threatened to claim him. She set the bottle aside, tossed a burping rag on her shoulder, and carefully maneuvered him until his head rested on the cloth. "No sleeping yet, sweet boy."

He fussed and whined, but she wouldn't be denied. Colic was not something she was ready to deal with. Not again. That had been a hard and painful lesson for both of them. She eased to her feet, supporting his neck as she stood, and began the gentle tapping against his back to help him release the air he'd swallowed. She carefully circled the room, quietly whispering to him and soothing him as she did.

"Shhh… Quiet, baby boy." He continued to fuss, but the sounds were gradually lessening with each pat and each careful step. "That's it, sweetheart."

She rubbed her nose against the light dusting of hair on his head, and breathed deeply. She always loved the scent of clean baby, a hint of powder and something sweet that every infant seemed to possess. Tears stung her eyes as memories of watching Lori do this exact thing filled her. Her best friend had been so overjoyed at becoming a mother… And then that was taken from her by Jack's own father.

A sob threatened to escape, but she pushed it down. She knew if Zane heard her crying, he would come running. He'd been hovering, constantly poking his head in and checking on her. Part of her ached to beg him to stay, but she knew her arrival and the trouble she brought with her could only be handled by him. He was running interference between his alpha and her, making sure she didn't have to speak before she was ready. She knew they were delaying the inevitable, but she appreciated the breathing room, nonetheless.

Jack's body went limp in her arms, his tiny weight completely relaxing against her chest, but she continued to slowly circle the room. She wasn't quite ready to let him go. She used him for comfort almost as much as he used her. For weeks it had been them against the crazy and cruel world, and now it seemed some of that was coming to an end. At least if Zane had his way.

The male was… scary. And sexy, her lioness readily interjected that descriptor. His body, his features, even the way he was so demanding appealed to her. And his possessiveness and that barely banked violence… It was as if God knew what she needed and handed it over on a silver platter.

Because she needed that uncontrollable violence to keep her safe, to keep Jack safe.

The muted ding of the front door's bell reached her, the sound slightly muffled due to the distance from the main area of the apartment. Lions had been coming and going all afternoon.

The deep rumble of the voices told her that quite a few men were within the space, and she only heard the occasional tinkling tone of a female. She imagined those two distinct voices belonged to the mates of the alpha and beta.

Addy sank into the large plush chair to the right of the door and let the soft cushions wrap around her in a welcoming embrace. She sighed and allowed herself to relax. It was the first time she'd been able to breathe without panic filling her since she'd begun her mad dash from Tony.

She let her eyes drift closed, blocking out the bright light in the room, and allowed herself to float toward sleep. She'd catch a quick nap since she knew Zane wouldn't be able to keep the pride leaders at bay forever.

Jack squirmed and she immediately stroked his small back in an effort to soothe him. "It's all right, baby boy."

Except it wasn't.

This time it wasn't the high-pitched doorbell that reached her, but the heavy thud of knuckles on wood announcing the visitor was banging on the main door. Which wasn't entirely odd. Not everyone used the doorbell after all. And yet… This person was granted entrance and the first stifled words from his mouth had her blood turning to ice and her heart freezing in her chest. The words weren't identifiable, but that voice…

She knew that voice. She'd heard it often enough. Every time she called Lori before moving to the city, that male answered. In every picture Lori sent her, that male hovered nearby. And—when Addy visited—everywhere they went, he followed. It was as if Lori couldn't breathe without him at her side. Now he was here. *Here* at her mate's home. Inside her mate's home. From what she recalled of the layout of Zane's apartment, the lion couldn't be more than one hundred feet from her at this very moment. No more than one hundred feet away from Jack.

It wasn't Tony, he was in prison, but that didn't mean he wasn't still involved in the running of the "business." The Colletti family—they could be put behind bars but they couldn't be taken down. Even though Tony's last name was Davis, he was a Colletti at heart.

Addy knew that Jennifer, the beta's mate, had put the human leader of the Colletti family in prison, and soon after it'd led to Tony's incarceration.

Yet he'd still kept after Lori and Jack. Or rather just Jack after the male orchestrated Lori's death.

Did they know she'd taken refuge with Zane? Was that why he was here?

The deep timbre of that voice grew closer, words exchanged between the dangerous male and Zane as they approached and she knew she had to get away. Somehow her mate was involved with this deadly and dangerous lion. Did he know who he'd let into his home? She prayed not. She prayed Zane wasn't somehow involved with Tony.

Her mind spun, thoughts pinging through her brain, and she finally snatched one from the rolling mass. Zane had recognized her fear and panic when she'd woken and had revealed there was more than one entrance and exit to the apartment. He'd probably told her to soothe her and she doubted he expected her to actually use the stairwell.

Well, she would. She would run from her mate despite her lioness' roar and scraping at Addy's mind. It wanted to remain and confront their mate, find out why he'd brought that male into his home. Except… She knew this intruding lion was fast, able to shift much quicker than Addy, and it would take him no more than one slice to tear out her throat. He could walk into the room, see she held Jack to her chest, and then kill her for stealing him. Three seconds tops and there was no telling what would happen to Jack after she died.

No, she couldn't risk it. She accepted running was probably a mistake and it was only a matter of time before Tony's men, or Zane himself, found her again, but she had to try. Lori entrusted Jack to her care because she knew Addy would do whatever it took to keep him safe.

She jumped from the chair and strode across the room to snatch up the diaper bag. She hadn't even touched it before that moment, but Zane assured her it carried all the "baby shit she needed." So she snared it, juggled Jack so she could place the strap across her chest, and then she held the baby tightly once again as she approached the door.

Ever so quietly she turned the knob and eased it open, allowing her attention to flick up and down the hallway. The area remained empty and she took her chance. She shot down the length, heading away from the main area of the apartment and straight to the last room.

She crept into the space, immediately heading for the closet. Once inside she made sure the door was closed behind her and then she focused on gaining access to the stairwell. The back wall looked exactly as he'd described, plain and flat, not hinting at what it concealed, but she knew better.

Addy poked and prodded at the left side, hunting for the panel that was supposed to slide apart at the touch of a werelion. The oils in her skin would identify her species. It was then she realized Zane was much taller than she was, so she needed to reach higher. The moment she extended her arm and skimmed her fingertips over the painted wall, the access panel she'd been hunting slid aside to reveal a keypad. She rubbed her fingers together, trying to remember the code that would grant her access.

"Come on, come on, come on…" Addy knew it, she did, but she couldn't remember dammit. "Stupid, stupid, stupid, what is it?"

A single squeak silenced her, piercing her chest like a knife, and she froze in place. It had been too clear, too close, and she accepted she was moments from being caught. Someone was nearby, whether Zane or another male, she didn't know. But they were *there*.

Then the scent struck her—evil, anger, violence… Distantly she recognized Zane's aroma as well, but it was the other that had adrenaline flooding her veins.

Fear pummeling her, she looked around the closet, hunting for a place to hide Jack. They were drawing closer with every second she hesitated. She glanced to her left and right and finally settled on placing him on the ground in the farthest corner of the space. She placed the diaper bag at his side, hopefully keeping him corralled and safe.

The moment he was out of harm's way, she centered herself in the closet. Allowing her lioness to come forward, golden fur slowly slid from her pores and coated her skin. Her human hands quickly transformed to deadly claws while her fangs lengthened and sharpened in preparation of tearing into flesh.

She wouldn't let the male have him. She would go down fighting and hopefully Zane would finish the job she started. She didn't believe her mate knew who he'd allowed into the space— he was rough and raw, but not evil. If the lion came after her, she had no doubt Zane would go at him.

*

"You don't need to follow me," Zane glanced over his shoulder at the other lion. In fact, he really didn't want the male anywhere near him while he completed his task.

"I was hoping you'd let me see that kid of yours." Kevin smiled and something about that grin rubbed him the wrong way. "I've got two nephews, and man, I just love the little ones."

Kevin could like all the little ones he liked, but he wasn't getting near Jack and Addy.

"I hear you." Zane nodded. "Why don't you head back to the living room? I'll see if I can coax Addy in a second." His phone had vibrated only moments ago, telling him someone had accessed the apartment's "back door." The only other person who knew of it was Addy and he couldn't help the anger and fear that battled inside him. She was his mate and was trying to leave him? He made sure Kevin remained near the room's door before he focused on the closet. "I just need to check—"

"I'll die before I let you have him."

The words punched him the chest and Zane fought to catch up, battled to figure out what had suddenly gone wrong. When he'd left Addy an hour ago, she'd been fine. She still hadn't wanted to come out and meet other enforcers, and he happily agreed. His lion didn't want any other males around her while she remained unclaimed. His fellow enforcer Oscar was a charmer, and the ladies always liked Lennox. He didn't want either of those men sniffing after his Addy.

So, how did they go from Addy lovingly cuddling Jack in one of the spare bedrooms to her facing off against him with death on her mind? He'd expected her to need a little calming and a few words that eased her worries as he led her back to the guestroom. She'd been running with Jack for a while. He should have anticipated her attempt at escape.

"Addy?" He held his hands up, palms out while raising his eyebrows in question. "What's going on, sweetheart?"

But her attention wasn't on him. No, it was slightly lower and over his left shoulder. She was focusing on Kevin. The male was a newcomer to the pride, previously living as a lone lion in the city and only recently requesting to join an organized pride. While Marcus handled the whole continent, he also kept things organized in their home city.

Kevin had been training as an enforcer for the last month and Marcus and Brett had slowly been feeling him out. The two males as well as Zane hadn't trusted him and it seemed that Addy felt the same way. However, this seemed a little extreme, even for him.

"Addy?" He took a half step forward.

"I mean it." She flexed her fingers, claws lengthening farther. The rapid snap and crack of bones preceded the transformation of her mouth to better resemble a lion's snout. That partial shift gave her more room for her cat's deadly teeth.

"Why don't you tell me what's wrong?" He sensed she was on the edge, her scent sinking into him and pure panic as well as utter terror stung his nose. "Addy—"

The rest of his thought didn't escape his lips because his world exploded in a rush of skin and fur.

Kevin snarled, the rage-filled sound striking Zane in the back and that was immediately followed by a rush of pain that consumed his left shoulder. Claws dug into his flesh and yanked, attempting to remove him from the doorway.

Fuck that shit.

No matter Kevin's history, no matter his strength, he was no match for Zane. He immediately threw off the other male's attack and spun in place to face his opponent. In that rush of movement, his transition equaled Kevin until it was partially shifted lion against partially shifted lion. Whatever Kevin's reason for attack, it would be the last thing he ever did.

His body flexed and strained as he fought the smaller lion. He roared and struck with his right hand, catching his opponent in the jaw. Skin and muscle split, exposing the bone beneath. Kevin tried to return the favor, but Zane easily blocked it and countered with a swipe across the chest, leaving deep furrows in his wake.

Red painted Kevin's skin and soaked into his clothing. It continued down and stained the wood as well.

Kevin backed off, retreating slightly, and Zane pushed his advantage. He stepped forward, going on the attack and went after the male.

Rage burned inside.

Zane and his lion demanded retribution. He could deal with an attack on himself, but this asshole went after his mate and that was unacceptable.

He locked claws with Kevin—arms and paws moving in a blur. Cut. Slice. Gouge. Pain assaulted him, but Zane pushed it aside. He didn't have time to worry about the hurt that covered him. The other lion's fury made his hatred for Addy easily evident and he knew only death would bring an end to this male's loathing for his mate.

Zane snarled and roared, threatening his opponent with sound as he continued his relentless attack. The heavy pounding of booted feet on wood reached him, but he couldn't spare a moment to focus on those who approached. No, he had a lion to kill. Until that was done, he had to keep his attention on Kevin.

The nearing newcomers made his opponent more desperate, made him make mistake after mistake, granting Zane opportunity after opportunity. Yes, he had his own peppering of cuts and bruises, but Zane saw the white of Kevin's bones almost as much as he saw the fresh red of his flesh.

"Zane!" Marcus yelled and then stepped forward to move between him and Kevin.

Rather than let the alpha put an end to the battle, Zane snapped at the male and swung his arm in a great arch, claws ready to sink into his leader's arm. "Mine!"

"Dammit, Zane!" Once again he ignored his alpha.

Jab. Duck. Feint. Swing.

More and more blood flowed as strength fled Kevin until one final punch scent him tumbling to the ground and sliding across the slick surface until he collided with the wall. Still Zane went after him. He rushed forward, intent on finishing the job he started, only to have arms and hands halt his progress.

"No, dammit," Brett snarled in his ear.

"Fucking quit it," Oscar demanded.

"God damn asshole." Lennox merely stated the truth.

All three men held him steady, refusing to let him go, and then his vision was consumed by Marcus. "What the fuck is your problem?"

His problem? *They* were his problem.

"Let Zane go!" Addy's trembling voice cut through their conversation and Zane's lion shifted his focus to their mate. "Let him—" his mate sobbed, "go."

Instead of fighting to get at Kevin, Zane changed his tactic and yanked backward against the three males. So surprised by his action, he easily slipped from their hold and was able to race to Addy's side. He immediately swept her into his arms, uncaring that his blood would soak into her clothing. If anything, it would warn others away from her. He hadn't claimed her yet, but now she was coated in his scent.

She wrapped her arms around him, clinging to him as tears soaked his skin and he immediately sought to ease her fears. "I'm fine. Everything's fine." She continued to cry, and he worried she'd make herself sick. "I'm okay, sweetheart, but what about Jack?"

"Jack…?" She sniffled. "He's—"

She lifted her head and as before she looked past his shoulder and stiffened, telling without words that someone approached.

He spun and faced off against the group that drew near her. Marcus took the lead while Brett, Oscar, and Lennox stood at his back. "You need to tell me what the hell is going on here. Now."

Zane would tell his alpha if he knew. The only thing he was conscious of was that Kevin tried to come after his mate.

Addy trembled against his back, her front pressed against his blood soaked clothing.

"I'm waiting," Marcus growled.

His mate shook once again, her fear pounding at him and his lion. That scent had him snarling anew. Which, in turn, had the four males returning the sounds.

"Zane," she whispered. "If... If they'll get Kevin out of here, I'll talk to them. But not—not with him here."

That had him stiffening and looking over his shoulder at her. "How do you know his name?"

"Because... he used to work for Tony Davis. And Tony Davis is Jack's father. He's the murderer who *disposed* of Jack's mother," she whimpered. "Kevin helped Tony kill her. He's been chasing me—"

For his involvement in Tony's world and the death of Jack's mother, the guy was gonna die. Because he'd actually been chasing Zane's mate, he was gonna die *now*.

He shrugged off Addy's hold and from one breath to the next, his shift rolled through him. He bowled past the four males, brushing them aside as if they didn't exist, and launched himself at the now unconscious Kevin.

Jaws spread wide, lion's teeth fully in place, and his mouth watered at the thought of tearing Kevin into pieces. He would start at the male's throat, ripping it out in one snap. No, wait he wanted to hear the male's screams. He wanted Kevin to fear death just as Addy had while she'd been on the run. Yes, that seemed like a wonderful idea. He'd start from the bottom. See if the male could chase anyone with no feet.

Best. Plan. Ever.

Except, just as he was about to crunch into Kevin's ankle, a larger feline body shoved him aside. Now he faced off against his own alpha, the massive lion outweighing him easily and Marcus would have no trouble putting him down. But Zane's cat wanted blood, it wanted yells of pain and to breathe the sweet scent of death.

Marcus bared his fangs in a clear threat and Zane snarled. He paced along the wall, eyes trained on his alpha as he fought to find any hint of vulnerability in the male's defense of Kevin. And he found nothing. *Dammit.*

Then one single sound drew away his aggression and replaced it with the fierce need to protect and guard. It didn't come from the alpha's or beta's mate, or even Addy. No, it came from Jack. Little Jack who couldn't yet defend himself and Zane's lion decided caring for the small child would fall onto his golden shoulders.

With one last curl of his lip at Marcus, he abandoned his post near the wall and padded toward Addy. He carefully nudged her deeper into the closet, and nosed the bag that kept Jack hidden. He gently pushed it aside with one paw and then met his mate's gaze. With a tilt of his head, he encouraged her to lift the baby and give it comfort. Did he want vengeance for what happened to Jack and Addy? Yes. But it could wait and explanations to the small group hovering in the doorway could wait. Right now he needed to care for his family.

CHAPTER FOUR

Addy stared down at the small child, little Jack snug and content in his new crib. The crib wasn't the only thing new. Somehow the pride had transformed one of Zane's spare bedrooms into a nursery within hours. The enforcers as well as the alpha and beta's mates all pitching in to create a space for Jack.

Part of her should be annoyed with the assumption she and the baby would be staying with Zane, but then the other part of her realized *of course* she would stay with Zane. He was her mate and no amount of drama or trouble could change that. So… here she was.

At least until the alpha—no, he wanted her to call him Marcus—made a decision about the baby. Lori had no family to speak of, but Tony had relatives—though the family was filled with men who thought someone spilling coffee on their shirt was a good reason to tear out the offender's throat. Which meant Marcus was torn between the laws of their people and what was best for Jack.

"He's not going to disappear on you," Zane murmured. "No one is taking him from us."

Her lioness purred, satisfied with both her mate's presence and his words. She slowly turned from the crib to face her mate. "I understand, but are you sure we're worth all this trouble?"

Zane moved faster than a bullet, closing the distance between them in what seemed like an instant, and then she was crushed to him. His fingers tangled in her hair, pulling her head back, while his other arm wrapped around her waist and held her close. "Yes," he hissed. "Protecting you both is never trouble." He leaned down and nuzzled her neck. "I want to do nothing but care for you and Jack for the rest of our lives."

"But—"

"You're mine. He's mine."

Tension she hadn't realized she'd been clinging to finally fled her body. She slumped against him and allowed him to take her weight. When he eased his fist, she released a heavy sigh and she leaned against his chest. She breathed deeply and drew his scent into her lungs.

"I know it's going to be hard. The Collettis—Davises—are going to try and take him. But Lori…" *Wants me to keep him out of that world.*

"They can try, but they won't succeed." This time, his touch wasn't rough, but very gentle as he encouraged her to lift her chin and meet his gaze. "Baby, you don't understand right now, but you will. What I take, what I claim, stays mine. Someday you'll believe that."

"I want to but…" She'd been running and hiding and knew what the Colletti family was capable of.

"You will." He lowered his head, his expression one of asking permission as he slowly brought his lips near her.

Zane was going to kiss her, or at least wanted to, and was waiting for her reaction. She only had one, of course. Despite her problems, despite the fact the Colletti family wanted her blood and Jack in their possession, she wanted to mate him.

He did not complete the kiss, did not press their lips together, but instead hovered above her mouth. He was still giving her a chance to say no.

"Is it safe? Will someone…"

Zane spoke against her mouth. "I would never do anything to risk your safety. The alpha and beta agreed to stand guard while new background checks are run on the alpha's guards and pride enforcers. But if you want to wait…"

If she wanted to wait, he'd give her time. Except she knew he wanted her, could feel evidence of his arousal and need hard against her hip and yet… He was giving her the chance to say no. She didn't know of any other male who'd be so understanding. And it was those words that made the decision for her.

"I—I trust you and if you say we're safe, then we are. Which means I don't want to wait." She pressed to her tiptoes, anxious to begin a kiss that would eventually lead to other more delicious things, but he didn't allow her to do so. She whimpered, and tried again, only to be thwarted.

"You were ready to leave me, Addy." His voice was hoarse and rough.

Shame washed over her, anger at herself over not trusting him pummeling her. She should have. She doubted she'd be given a mate who meant her harm.

Instinctively she knew the man holding her didn't have an evil bone in his body. Her time with Lori had allowed her to fine-tune her senses.

Addy opened her mouth to release the apology that hovered on her lips only to have him immediately silence any regret.

"No, don't say anything. It was smart. You didn't know me—*don't* know me—and had to keep Jack safe. I admit it hurt my pride a little, but I can't deny you did a good thing." A fierce possessiveness filled his gaze. "But now you know I'm worthy of your trust. So if you even think about running again I will take you over my knee and turn that sexy ass of yours bright red."

She couldn't have stopped the blush that filled her face had she tried. "You can't say things like that."

"Why?" He raised a single brow. "It's the truth."

With a groan, she nudged him. "I'm sure you *think* you'll do that but—"

"Oh, it'll happen." Zane breathed deeply and released a rumbling purr. "And I think you like that idea. You want me to strip—"

She placed her fingers over his lips to shut him up. She wasn't going to confess that it intrigued her. Not at all, not ever. And *especially* not in Jack's nursery. "Hush. Don't you know there's an infant not three feet away?"

He didn't even bother apologizing. "What?" He shrugged. "It's not like the kid isn't going to hear and see us loving on each other at some point."

…loving on each other…

"Loving… Our son sure as hell isn't going to see—"

"I like hearing you calling him our son, but you shouldn't curse around him. Don't want to teach him bad habits." His voice turned husky and seductive. "And he won't watch us loving, but he's going to know his parents make love. I bet you're a screamer. Am I right?" He shook his head. "Don't answer that, I'll find out myself."

Zane released her and turned away, snatching her wrist and tugging her from the room. He drew her down the hallway, their steps quiet as their bare feet padded toward the master bedroom. It wasn't a far walk from the nursery down the hallway, but it seemed like a million miles. And once again, he practically read her mind. The moment they stepped into the room they'd share, he pointed to one of the bedside tables. "I bought the best baby monitor they make. You can listen to him, but it's got a camera too so you can see him as well. If he makes a sound or breathes funny, we'll know."

And she found herself tumbling toward loving him all the more.

The presence of the monitor reminded her of what he'd said. "Parents? You said parents making love…"

He jolted to a stop. "Of course. What else can we be? I already told you you're not leaving me. Don't even think—"

"No," she shook her head. "I wasn't... I didn't think... we're parents. We hardly know each other and we're parents."

"Exactly. And now, we need to give Jack a brother or sister." He slowly drew her toward the massive king-size bed. "Any objections?"

Yes, she had worries and concerns that still nagged her brain, but there could never be anything wrong with claiming her mate. "No, none at all."

*

Zane nearly pounced on her the moment the words registered. Instead, he tugged a bit harder and the moment she was close enough, he wrapped his arms around her and fell onto the bed. A bright laugh escaped her and he found himself smiling in response. Despite recent events, he was thrilled they could find a little bit of joy in each other. There was no doubt they needed it.

He rolled them, pinning her beneath his bulk and holding her captive. He managed to grasp her wrists in one hand and stretch her arms above her. With a firm but gentle push he pinned them in place. "Keep them there."

Addy whimpered and the sound went straight to his groin, making him twitch and throb in his jeans. He'd been hard for her the moment her scent filled him, and he'd been craving her ever since. Now, he'd have her.

"Addy? Are you listening?" When she released a low whine and nodded, he moved on.

The feel of her, the sensation of having those curves flush against him, had so many fantasies flitting through his mind. He wished they had time to spend days mating and exploring each and every one of his ideas. But they didn't, they had Jack to worry about and care for. So that made each coming together important. He had time for one idea, not thirty-seven.

At her confirmation, he released her wrists and got to the task of discovering his mate's secrets.

He captured her mouth in a passionate kiss, sliding his tongue between her lips and exploring her with a single sweep. Her flavors blossomed across his taste buds, arousing him even further as the flavors of sweetness and heat filled him. She teased him, carefully sucking on his tongue, and he nearly came from that alone. He carefully drew his mouth away and nipped her lower lip.

"Witch," he whispered into her mouth. She merely hummed and wiggled against him, forcing a groan from his chest. "You're gonna kill me."

Then he focused on making her cry out, torturing her with pleasure as she was now doing to him.

When he asked for his lion's help, the beast was quick to react and transform Zane's fingernails to sharpened claws so he could slice away her clothing. Delicious inches of her flesh were revealed, goose bumps rising on the newly exposed skin, and his mouth watered with the need to sample her.

He wasn't one to deny himself, so he slid down her body, licking every bit of her that was bared. He lapped at her collarbone, nibbled her nipple, and when he got to the juncture of her thighs he nuzzled her slightly damp curls. The salty musk of her arousal filled his nose and despite the gentle tightening of her legs in an effort to hide from him, he refused to let her. Even when small claw-tipped fingers pricked his skull, he remained in place. He did, however, let his attention meet hers and he narrowed his eyes.

"Where are your hand supposed to be?"

"Zane…"

He puffed a warm burst of air over her needy flesh. "What, love?"

"It's… I'm not pretty… down there…"

No, she wasn't pretty, she was gorgeous. The plump lower lips, the swollen pinkness of her need for him… Magnificent. And his. Couldn't forget that part.

"Shhh… You're more than pretty and right here… this is glorious." He kept his attention on her as he lowered his head and pressed a soft kiss to the seam of her sex lips. "I'm going to taste you, make you scream my name, and then I'm going to mate you." As each word left his mouth, her breathing increased until she panted and squirmed. "Any objections?" Addy shook her head and he smiled wide. "Good."

Then he did exactly that. He put his mouth against her, tongue sliding out to lap at her cream as he gathered the evidence of her need into him. The flavors overwhelmed him with their strength and intensity, calling to his inner beast and demanding the lion come forward.

He wanted to roll and bathe in her scent until he was covered from head to toe.

He suckled her clit, the very source of her pleasure, and moved with her as she rocked against him. She babbled and moaned, begging for more. When he traced her opening with a single finger, she whimpered, but when he slid two fingers into her velvety warmth, she finally screamed. She milked his intrusion, hips moving with him as he thrust and retreated, and all the while he continued flicking that bundle of nerves with his tongue.

Her face flushed and her eyes went glassy. He'd done that, he'd overwhelmed his mate until she was a trembling mass of need, and yeah, he was cocky about that fact.

Zane knew she was close, the intricacy of her flavors telling him she'd moved beyond a craving for him and on to bone deep need. A need he was happy to satisfy. When she began tightening around him rhythmically, he knew she lingered at the edge, that it wouldn't take much to send her into the abyss of joy.

He didn't stop his hand, but he did lift his mouth from her, smiling widely when she sobbed and gave him an accusing glare. "Do

you want to come now or with me inside you?"
Zane ached for her to pick the latter option. He
wanted to be hilt deep in her wetness and feel
her come apart around him. He slid his fingers
free and then carefully thrust into her once
again. "Addy?"

*

Zane wanted her to think? To *speak*? He had to
be kidding. Since he was no longer pushing her
toward the edge of release and instead had her
hovering near the brink, she figured he was
serious. Bastard.

He pushed deep once again, fingers curled and
stroking that pretty, pretty spot and she
shouted her decision to the ceiling. "Inside
me!"

Those three syllables had him bolting into
action. While it'd only taken moments for him
to slice and remove the clothing from her body,
he took even less time with his own. He'd
hardly left her before he was back, his sweat
dampened flesh firm against her and the skin
on skin connection had her inner lioness
purring and aching to bare its belly to their
mate.

He resettled between her thighs, but instead of his mouth floating above her center, it was his hardness pressed intimately against her. He gently rocked his hips, sending a lightning bolt of pleasure down her spine and she shuddered, unable to squash her reaction to his touch.

She wanted him, there was no denying that, but she didn't want it going to his head either.

"You like that?" He rolled his hips once again and she smiled when her shudder was answered by his own.

"I think we both do." She smiled widely. Zane growled, baring his teeth in mock anger and she was quick to respond. "Don't flash 'em unless you're using 'em."

That caused him to growl once again and she smiled even wider. Her teasing hit the mark, and now he was serious. His hands were everywhere, stroking and petting her, lips gliding over her skin and sucking on her. In all the while, his hardness lay flush with her heat until she was ready to scream with the need for him.

"Dammit, Zane…"

He rumbled and she had the distinct feeling it was actually a laugh. Her suspicion was confirmed when he lifted his head from her breast and met her stare. "Yeah, baby?"

"Quit teasing. You gave me a choice and I told you I wanted to come with you inside me. That can't happen if you don't, you know, get *inside* me."

She was pretty sure that part was obvious.

Another chuckle as he carefully lifted his hips enough to position the tip of his length against her moist entrance. He carefully teased her, sliding in a bare inch before retreating.

"Is this what you want?"

She whimpered and nodded.

"Nope, give me the words."

"Bastard." She shuddered and swallowed the moan that leapt to her lips. "Yes, that's what I want. I want you inside me."

"Then that's what you'll have."

And damn the man, he kept his promises. His hardness carefully slid inside her, stretching her as his fingers had not, and she moaned with the new pain-tinged pleasure that overtook her. He slipped deeper and deeper, his length stroking her and she trembled with the overwhelming sensations of his possession.

He set a maddening rhythm, a careful retreat met by a gentle thrust that did nothing more than make her crazy with need for him. They remained quiet, their bodies and breathing making more than enough sound. Their hips met, each collision pushing her closer to the ultimate joy, and her body called for release.

She hovered at the edge, dangling on the very precipice, and she held her breath as she waited to see if he'd give her what she needed.

Like any good mate, he met her needs. He flashed his white lengthened fangs, his lion obviously prepared to claim her, and Addy found her lioness responded in kind.

"You're mine." The words spurred her pleasure, sending it sliding through her veins and it snatched away any hint of control that remained.

She was nothing more than a ball of overwhelming sensation and soul deep need.

"You're mine." She bared her fangs as well, letting him know what was to come.

Based on the flare of gold in his eyes, she knew he more than embraced the idea. They became a mass of writhing bodies, both hunting for that ultimate release. Their roars and yells gained in volume with each passing second. His were a constant demand while hers a steady plea for more. Until finally…

Finally the end was there. Her orgasm overtook her in a surprising wave of blinding ecstasy. Her body was no longer her own, but merely a rolling wave of bliss. She trembled and twitched, toes curling and limbs refusing to acknowledge her commands, but there was one thing she could do.

Addy could claim him. Because as he lowered his head, mouth wide and prepared to sink into her flesh, she did the same. She struck as he bit her, going deep and she reveled in the coppery sweetness that rolled over her tongue. Heaven, more and more heaven filled her as she sucked on the wound she'd caused. Pain assaulted her as well, telling her she now belonged to him.

The evidence of their mating continued, her very essence reaching out for his, the glowing ethereal tendrils twining and tying them together. They would forever be linked, mind to mind until their thoughts were no longer their own. There would be no secrets from her mate. His thickness grew even more, knotting their bodies as his release filled her. They would be tied together, body and soul, this reaction only present between true mates, and she gloried in this cascade of events.

She was his, and he was hers. They'd shared those words, but now they were connected forever in truth and nothing could ever tear them apart. And now his mating knot would ensure they remained close for minutes after they'd satisfied each other. It wasn't a time to be rushed or shortened, but a time of connection for a couple.

Except… the soft wail of an infant through a baby monitor had Zane softening in an instant. It was as if nature programmed a parent's body to…

But they weren't parents. Not in truth. But in her heart, obviously in Zane's heart, they were. *If only…*

CHAPTER FIVE

Addy wasn't sure what to expect. They'd simply received a call, Colton informing that Marcus requested their presence at the pride's lands situated an hour outside the city. Zane hadn't yet taken her to the area, his concern for their safety keeping him close to home and Addy and Jack within the apartment unless they had enforcers at their side.

She couldn't blame her mate for his caution. Things in the city were still very much in the air. The Collettis—human and werelion—were still a big threat despite the leaders being in prison. Criminal life apparently didn't end behind bars. It simply meant the men had to be more creative.

But something had to have changed if Zane was willing to take them to such a wide open and hard to protect area.

Their SUV carefully bounced over the rutted road, each rise and fall dragging giggles and laughs from Jack. He'd grown so much in the month they'd been with Zane, as if love and care were all he needed to blossom into a healthy and happy cub.

The trees that had surrounded them for the last twenty minutes finally thinned out and then completely vanished, exposing a large area of flat, cleared land. Numerous cars were parked off to one side, many familiar to her. She recognized that Marcus and Brett were there, but also several other enforcers she'd come to know as well. *Lennox, Grant, Austin…*

"Are we having a pride gathering?" She furrowed her brow.

"Not that I know of." Zane seemed as confused as her.

Jack continued giggling and enjoying himself as they carefully pulled up alongside the alpha's vehicle. The second her mate shifted into park, the baby began fussing and yelling to be released. He didn't mind being in the car, but *only* when it was moving.

"I know, I know, I'm coming…" Addy quickly hopped from the SUV and went toward the back seat only to have Zane cut her off.

She shook her head and smiled. The big, bad enforcer was a sucker for a baby. "Come to daddy, big man."

Leaving her mate to it, she stepped back and looked around the space. She spied the small group near the tree line, several of the males in their lion form, while others remained on two feet. She recognized Jennifer and Penelope, and noted what seemed to be hardly suppressed excitement surrounding the women. She wasn't sure what had the lionesses on pins and needles—there was no telling with them. They bounced around over a night on the town and new baby booties in equal measure.

Zane's large hand settled on her lower back and she glanced at him to see he cuddled Jack to his chest with his free arm. As a family they padded toward the group and with each step, her worry grew. Yes, the two women seemed to be brimming with anticipation, but the men's gazes were more shuttered which added to her unease.

"Zane?"

He leaned over and pressed a kiss to her temple. "We're fine."

Fine. Right. Of course.

Soon they were mere feet from the group, and the delicious scent of fresh meat teased her nose. That was also about the time she realized the few lion males were busily cleaning themselves and licking their whiskers. A recent kill. They couldn't be delivering bad news if they'd been hunting for celebratory food, right? Unless it was an apology meal because Marcus finally came to a decision about Jack.

She flicked her attention to the large alpha and swallowed hard. An unreadable yet serious expression covered his features and a hint of fear snaked its way through her body.

Jack fussed and Zane rubbed her back. "Calm down. Everything's fine," he murmured.

As they approached the small group, Penelope broke away and rushed toward them, her arms outstretched. "Oh, let me snuggle and get my baby fix."

Addy looked from the alpha's mate to Marcus and then Zane, hunting for any hint of an ulterior motive. She didn't see any subterfuge and yet… And yet Addy couldn't shake the feeling that something huge was in the works. And that something involved Jack.

Acting as only a mama lion could, she darted away from Zane and immediately cut Penelope off with a low snarl and curl of her lip. "What's going on?"

Penelope drew up short, sliding to a stop before crashing into Addy, and the woman stared at her, head tilted to the side in question. "What do you mean?" Marcus approached and took up position at Penelope's side. "We kept things small because you don't trust everyone in the pride yet, but we wanted to celebrate—"

Marcus nudged his mate behind him and Addy spied a glare on Penelope's face—the expression directed at the alpha—before she was hidden from view.

"Celebrate?" Zane tugged Addy back and carefully passed her the baby and then she was staring at his back so the males faced each other. "What are we celebrating? Why are we out here?" Some of the concern she'd held through their travels now seemed to be making an impression on Zane. "What's going on?"

"Of course we're celebrating." Marcus' tone left the 'idiot' hanging in the air. "Why the hell do you think I dragged you out here? Didn't Colton tell you that I—"

A movement off to her left drew her attention and she watched as one of the larger males carefully rose to his feet and inched toward the tree line.

"Colton told me to get my family here by four. He didn't tell me why," Zane snarled. "He's left us on edge all day. So what's going on?"

That distant lion continued on his careful path.

"He should have explained that I met with Tony Davis and we've all come to an agreement that Jack Davis is now Jack Edwards. His official parents are Zane and Addy Edwards. In exchange, he gets transferred to a better facility and we stop pressuring him to snitch on others." Marcus finished his statement with a wide smile and she wondered if that was *all* Marcus promised. "That's why we're here." Marcus shook his head. "He didn't tell you, did he? Dammit." Marcus' gaze remained on Zane and he tilted his head back to yell. "Colton, get up here." The alpha peered around Zane and met Addy's gaze. "I'm sorry if he caused you to worry. Colton probably thought he was playing a joke and that it be funny to keep you in the dark."

Addy was slowly realizing the stress she'd carried all day was only because some overgrown adolescent thought he was amusing. Now her fear was slowly turning to anger and she recognized that the furball attempting to get away with his tail tucked between his legs and head hanging low was probably the "Colton" in question.

"I think he's trying to disappear." Addy gestured toward the now disappearing male.

A low growl escaped and then her mate was snapping questions at Marcus. "Jack is ours?"

"Yes."

"And everyone knew this? Colton, too?"

"Yes."

"So he was trying to cause trouble on purpose?"

"It appears so."

She could practically read her mate's mind and knew he was a balloon of aggression just waiting to pop. Zane did not take it well when others upset her, and today's events definitely qualified as an 'upset.'

"One last question." Zane tilted his head from side to side, cracking his neck. "Can you look after my family while I take care of something for a minute?"

Marcus' response was instantaneous. "Of course."

Zane spun around to face her and dropped a soft kiss to the top of Jack's head before then placing those lips over hers in a brief touch. "I'll be right back, baby. I gotta take care of something real quick."

Then he was gone, racing into the trees. He ripped clothes free of his body as he went and was fully transformed before he hit the forest. Roars, snarls, and growls reached past the trees but otherwise the battle was hidden from view.

Penelope and Jennifer rushed forward, the Alpha Mate easily pushing Marcus aside, and both women spouted reassurances that Zane would come back to her hale and whole. There was nothing to worry about. Sometimes the enforcers needed to let off a little steam. A lot of times Colton needed his ass handed to him.

Addy let it rush in one ear and out the other because truly, she wasn't worried a bit. She'd find out the details about Tony's relinquishment of Jack later, but she trusted the alpha to be speaking the truth. He wasn't the alpha of North America for no reason. No, her mind was whirling around a handful of words from her mate.

…my family…

A loud booming roar shook the earth and she recognized Zane's frustration. Jack giggled in response, squirming in her hold, and she couldn't help but smile along with the baby.

Yes, they made up a small family and hopefully it would grow someday. Actually, she lightly brushed her lower stomach, it would grow very, very soon.

THE END

If you enjoyed this book, please be totally awesomesauce and leave a review so others may discover it as well. Long review or short, your opinion will help other readers make future purchasing decisions. So, go forth and rate my level-o-awesome!

By the way... below is a list of the books in the Quick & Furry series:

Quick & Furry #1: Chasing Tail
Quick & Furry #2: Tailing Her
Quick & Furry #3: On Her Tail
Quick & Furry #4: Heads or Tails

ABOUT THE AUTHOR

Ex-dance teacher, former accountant and erstwhile collectible doll salesperson, New York Times and USA Today bestselling author Celia Kyle now writes paranormal romances for readers who:

1) Like super hunky heroes (they generally get furry)
2) Dig beautiful women (who have a few more curves than the average lady)
3) Love laughing in (and out of) bed.

It goes without saying that there's always a happily-ever-after for her characters, even if there are a few road bumps along the way.

Today she lives in Central Florida and writes full-time with the support of her loving husband and two finicky cats.

If you'd like to be notified of new releases, special sales, and get FREE eBooks, subscribe here: http://celiakyle.com/news

You can find Celia online at:

http://celiakyle.com
http://facebook.com/authorceliakyle
http://twitter.com/celiakyle

COPYRIGHT PAGE

Made in the USA
Columbia, SC
12 January 2020